THE
BUNNY TALES
COLLECTION

INTRODUCTION

You don't often see a bunny by herself. That is because bunnies like nothing better than being together, snuggling up in their warm burrows as one big, happy family. Of course, those burrows can be pretty noisy places, with everyone trying to talk at once.

Bunnies love to tell stories, and you can read some of them in this book. They are all about the bunnies who live in Warren Wood, far away beneath the great oak tree.

Do you know what happens when a bunny eats too much fudge? Or gets too friendly with a fox? Or tries to make a wedding dress at the very last minute?

Read this collection of bunny stories and you will soon find out. If you look very carefully at the pictures, you will find lots of hidden surprises there, too.

Pictures tell stories too from age to age;
If you search you may spot
One carrot (or a lot!)
Hidden on every page.

THE
BUNNY
TALES
COLLECTION

Illustrated by
CATHIE SHUTTLEWORTH

Written by
NICOLA BAXTER

ARMADILLO

For Hugh Shrive

C.A.S.

First published 1999 by Armadillo Books
An imprint of
Bookmart Limited
Registered Number 2372865
Trading as Bookmart Limited
Desford Road, Enderby
Leicester LE9 5AD
England

ISBN 1-90046-587-6

Reprinted 2000

Produced for Bookmart Limited by Nicola Baxter
PO Box 215
Yelverton
Norwich
NR14 7UR

Editorial consultant: Ronne Randall
Designer: Amanda Hawkes

Printed in Italy

CONTENTS

Great-Uncle Otto's Tale of
THE BIG BAD BUNNY

One morning, the little bunnies were being unusually annoying. When they bounced on Great Uncle Otto's chair and broke the springs, that very wise old rabbit sighed and decided enough was well and truly enough.

"You young bunnies should be careful," he warned, waving his willow walking stick. "If you're not careful, you'll find yourselves in a very sticky situation indeed, just like the Big Bad Bunny."

"Oh, tell us, tell us!" called Pickles and Penny and all the other little bunnies.

"Very well," said Great-Uncle Otto, "but first you must find a cushion to put in my poor old chair and then you must sit absolutely still."

The little rabbits hurried to get ready. They loved the old rabbit's stories.

"The big bad bunny," Great-Uncle Otto began, "was once just an ordinary naughty little bunny—like you!"

The little bunnies wriggled in their seats, and Great-Uncle Otto went on.

"As this particular naughty bunny got older," he said, "he also got bigger and badder, until he was a very big, very bad bunny indeed."

"What did he do?" squealed Pickles.

"He tied his sister's shoelaces together, so she fell over. He ate his brother's birthday cake *before* that poor little bunny's birthday. He shut his mother in the pantry while he made mud pies on the living room carpet. He put jelly in his father's slippers. He gathered a bunch of flowers for his auntie . . . from her own garden. He filled the bathtub with frogs and put worms in the kitchen sink. Need I say more?"

"Oooh!" said the little bunnies. "He *was* bad, wasn't he?"

"He was," said Great-Uncle Otto gravely, "but, as I said, he found himself in a sticky situation. Oh yes, a very sticky situation indeed."

"What happened?" squeaked Penny.

"Honey," replied her great-uncle briefly.

"Honey?"

"Yes, honey. One day, his mother left a big jar of honey on the table when she went shopping. Of course, the big bad bunny wanted to taste it. He dipped in one paw. Then that greedy bunny dipped in two paws. But, you know, that honey was very thick and gloopy. He found that his paws were completely stuck!

And when he bent his head to try to pull out his paws, his ears got stuck to the sticky jar as well! Of course, he struggled, and when his mother came home, she found him with the jar on his head and one ear and two paws stuck inside it, while gloopy, golden honey trickled slowly down his face. He was not a happy bunny."

"And was he good after that?" asked Pickles.

"He was," said Great-Uncle Otto firmly. "He became a fine, upstanding bunny, kind, er . . . wise, and respected by all. Now run along and play and let me read my book."

"What was the big bad bunny's name?" asked Penny, as the little bunnies ran out of the door.

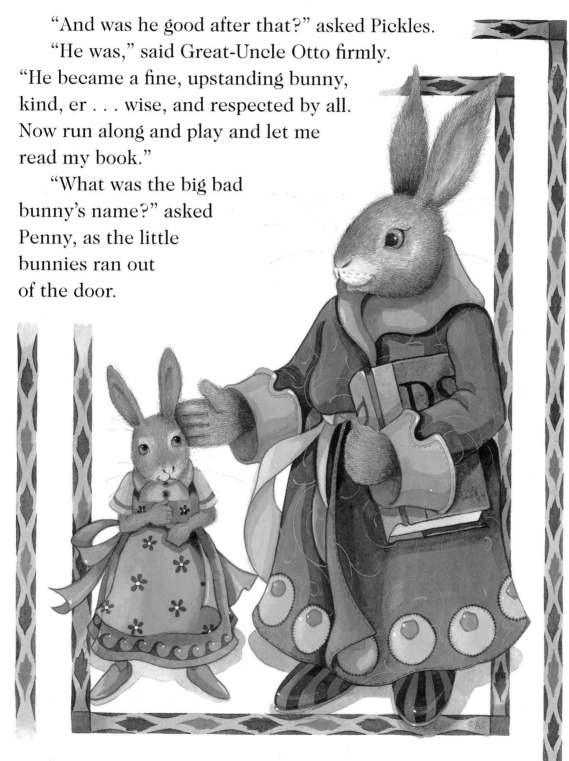

"Hrrrmph!" grunted her great-uncle. "Well, he happened to be called . . . *ahem* . . . Otto!"

Aunt Amelia's Tale of

The Funny Bunny

Rain was falling steadily in Warren Wood. The little bunnies looked miserably at the puddles forming near the entrance to the burrow. There would be no playing outside today.

"What can we do?" asked Whistler. "Hide and seek? Chase the bunny? I-spy?"

"Oh no," groaned Merry, "we've played those hundreds of times. We could tell jokes, though."

"I don't know any jokes," grumbled Pickles.

"Don't you?" said an amused voice from behind the sofa. It was Aunt Amelia, who had been picking up the tiny bits of thread she had dropped when she was doing her embroidery. "I know lots of jokes," said the surprising aunt. "They were told to me by a very funny bunny. He made everyone laugh so much that their ears went wobbly. I still know lots of his jokes."

"Like what?" asked Penny, suspiciously. In her experience, a grown-up rabbit's idea of what was funny was often very odd.

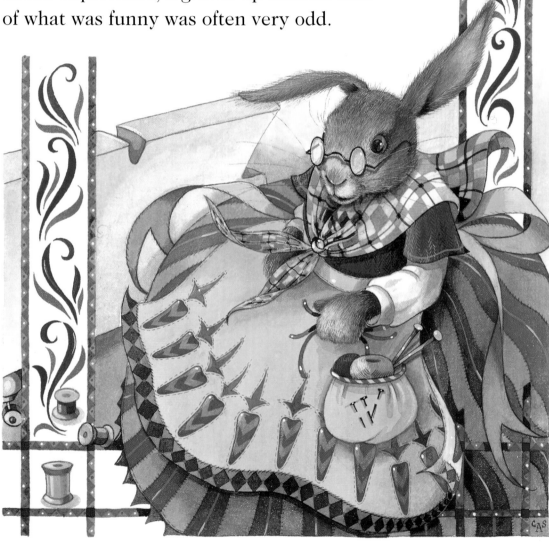

"Er . . . well, did you hear about the bunny who chopped down a tree, sawed it up, and made a car out of it?"

"No," said Pickles slowly.

"It wooden go!" chortled Aunt Amelia.

"Why not?" asked Penny.

"No, no, you don't understand!" cried her aunt. "The car was made of *wood* and it *wooden* go!"

A deafening silence greeted this statement. Clearly, the little bunnies didn't think it was funny at all.

"All right," said Aunt Amelia, searching her memory for another good joke. "Here's one. How can you tell if there's an elephant in a cupboard?"

"What's an efelant?" asked baby Bubbles.

Once this was explained, Aunt Amelia started her joke all over again. She sensed that her very best jokes were not going as well as she had hoped.

"I don't know," sighed Pickles. "How can you tell if there's an elephant in a cupboard?"

"Ha ha! Because the door won't shut!" crowed Aunt Amelia, her face quite pink with giggling.

The little bunnies looked at each other. This was really dreadful. But there was no stopping the embarrassing aunt.

"What do you give a sick bird?"

"What sort of bird?" asked Whistler.

"It doesn't matter what sort of bird." Aunt Amelia was beginning to get tetchy.

"Could it be a duck?"

"No, it couldn't be a duck, but it could be any kind of small bird."

"Why is it sick?" asked baby Bubbles.

"I don't know why it's sick," said Aunt Amelia faintly, "but what would you give it, anyway?"

"That depends on why it was sick," explained Penny. "If it had eaten too much, you wouldn't give it food, but if it hadn't eaten for days, you would, you see."

But Aunt Amelia was already halfway out of the room.

"I can see that the funny bunny's jokes are too sophisticated for you little ones," she sniffed. "I'm going to lie down."

When she had gone, the little bunnies forgot all about the jokes and had a lively game of hip-hop-ho until it was time for supper and bed.

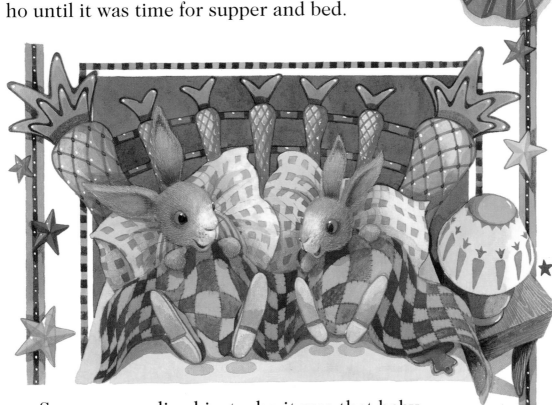

So no one realized just why it was that baby Bubbles woke up the next morning with a smile all over his face, saying, "Tweetment!"

Father Rabbit's Tale of

THE
CARROT COLLECTION

Tempers in the Big Burrow became a little frayed when Penny and Pickles started collecting things. They had a friend who collected postcards, but they thought that was pretty boring. Both of them wanted to collect something much more exciting than that.

"I'm going to collect leaves," said Penny. "They're really interesting, and there are lots of different kinds."

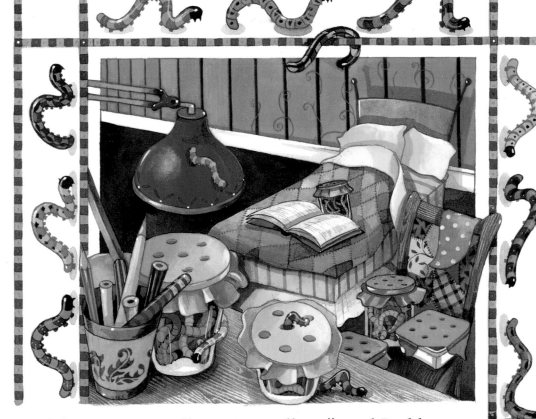

"I'm going to collect caterpillars," said Pickles. "There are lots of different kinds of them too, and they can crawl, you know, which is much, much more exciting."

"Hmmm," Penny was not so sure. Dimly in the back of her mind, she felt that there might be a problem if lots of caterpillars started crawling around in the Big Burrow. But it was impossible to change Pickles' mind once he had decided on something. Before long, every corner of his bedroom was filled with little jars and pots, covered with paper lids in which Pickles had carefully punched little holes.

"I hope you're giving those caterpillars plenty to eat," said Father Rabbit, looking suspiciously at the jars. "Caterpillars who are hungry might have a tendency to roam."

But Pickles took very good care of his caterpillars. In fact, he was so interested in them that he didn't even notice what Penny was doing.

Unfortunately, the day came when it was raining so hard that Pickles couldn't go outside to find leaves for his creepy-crawly friends. He was beginning to get desperate when he noticed a pile of leaves in the corner of the hallway outside the dining room.

"Those will be fine," said Pickles.

It was not until that evening, when Pickles' caterpillars had done quite a bit of chomping and chewing, that Penny was heard to shout from the middle of the burrow, "Who's moved my leaf collection?" Pickles hid under the bed for a very long time.

Next morning, it seemed that Pickles, too, had troubles. Each one of his caterpillars had turned into a hard, shiny thing that didn't move at all. Pickles left all his jars open in disgust.

"I can't understand you young rabbits," said Father Rabbit, when he saw the two little ones sitting sadly on the stairs. "In my day we used to collect something useful . . . like carrots! Why, I remember having the biggest and best carrot collection in all of Warren Wood. Let me tell you about it. Storage was the biggest problem, but I had a clever idea. . . ."

Now this was not the first time that the little rabbits had heard about Father Rabbit's famous carrot collection, and they were very sorry indeed that they'd given him the opportunity to tell them about it all over again. There were even photographs of the collection, which he eagerly dug out of a drawer. Between you and me, there are few things more boring than photographs of carrots, especially photographs of *hundreds* of carrots in rows. The carrot stories went on for days.

Finally, the little rabbits could stand it no longer. "Er . . . I must go and clear up my bedroom," said Pickles, which was such an unusual thing for him to say that Penny fell off her chair in surprise. But when she had picked herself up, she half remembered that she had promised to help Pickles, and she hurried off to join him.

And when the rabbits opened the door of Pickles' bedroom, they had the most wonderful surprise. Every one of the hard, shiny things had hatched . . .

into a beautiful, fluttering butterfly.

Grandma Molly's Tale of
THE TREETOP BUNNY

The annoying thing about kites is that they have a habit of getting stuck in trees. One breezy spring day, Penny and Pickles were as careful as they could be with their new kite. But when your mother has told you not to go very far from home, and your home is under a tree, accidents are bound to happen. Before long, the kite was hopelessly tangled, high in the branches.

Pickles at once tried to climb up to reach the balloon. But bunnies are not very good at climbing. He was only a little way from the ground before he too got stuck.

When Grandma Molly came out for some fresh air, she was surprised to see a kite *and* a rabbit dangling from different branches.

"Why, don't tell me you're going to take after your great-great-great-great-uncle Ebenezer, Pickles!" she cried.

Pickles was so interested in the idea of a great-great-great-great-uncle that he forgot to hold on and came down to earth with a *bump!*

"Who was *he*?" asked the little bunny, rubbing his bottom.

"I'll tell you about him," said Grandma Molly, "to take your mind off your . . . er . . . unmentionable bits."

Penny and Pickles giggled, but they settled down to hear the story.

"Ebenezer," said Grandma, "was a very strange bunny. He always wanted to be somewhere *high*. When he was a tiny baby, he would try to climb up onto the table. When he was older, he would balance on the tops of doors. *Very* dangerous. And when he was older still, he realized that trees were the tallest things around, and he wanted more than anything to go to live in a house at the top of a tree."

"But only birds live in trees!" said Penny.

"And bees," Pickles reminded her. He had had a rather painful experience the year before.

"Yes, indeed," replied Grandma Molly, "but that didn't stop Ebenezer. He tried to climb every tree he could. Unfortunately, as you've found, Pickles, bunnies are not good at climbing trees. They're very good at jumping but not very good at climbing. Even Ebenezer, who had had a lot of practice, found it difficult."

"What did he do?" breathed Penny.

"He didn't know what to do," said Grandma, "until his little cousin had a birthday party. One of the little bunnies was almost carried away by a balloon. Then Ebenezer knew how to get to the top of the tree."

"With a balloon?"

"Well, he needed more than one balloon, of course, but yes, that was his idea. That very afternoon, Ebenezer held onto a huge bunch of balloons and floated into the air. Up, up, up he went until. . ."

"Yes?" said Pickles.

"Yes?" cried Penny.

"The balloons touched the leaves of the tree."

"That didn't matter, did it?" asked Pickles, looking at the smooth edge of a leaf that had been stuck in his ears.

"Ah," said Grandma, "but this was not an oak tree, or an ash, or a maple. It was a holly tree!"

"They have really sharp leaves," squeaked Penny.

"*Pop! Pop! Pop! Pop!* The balloons burst one by one, and Ebenezer fell with a *bump!* onto a broad branch."

"How did he get down?" asked Pickles, thinking of his own painful fall.

"He didn't," said Grandma. "He liked it so much that he stayed up there. You know, sometimes when I catch sight of those mischievous little animals called squirrels, I can't help wondering if they are related to old Ebenezer."

Can you see some squirrels watching Penny and Pickles right now, high up in the branches? What do you think?

Cousin Hoppity's Tale of
THE BEST BIRTHDAY

When it was almost time for Pickles' birthday, nobody had any peace. Pickles was determined to have the biggest and best birthday that had ever been seen in Warren Wood. But what should it be like? Ever since he had been to Billy Bunny's Pirate Party, Pickles felt that a party should have a theme. He just couldn't decide what his should be.

"How about Dragons and Princesses?" said Penny, who liked the idea of dressing up as a beautiful princess.

"I don't want to be a dragon," said Pickles.

"How about Fairies and Elves?" suggested Penny. A fairy costume would be good, too.

"My ears are big enough, without pretending to be an elf," replied Pickles. "And anyway, Jimble already had one of those for his birthday last year. It would look as if I was copying."

Every day, Pickles worried about his party.

He was still worrying a few days later, when Cousin Hoppity came to stay.

Cousin Hoppity lived in a wood that was even wilder than Warren Wood and had a large river flowing through it. He was always full of stories of the adventures he had had. Pickles was secretly envious of him, but he always pretended to enjoy the calmer life under the oak tree.

"When it comes to birthdays," said Cousin Hoppity, "I'm the rabbit you want to ask. On my very best birthday, I didn't even *have* a party."

Despite himself, Pickles heard his own voice asking to hear the story. Hoppity was only too glad to begin.

"My birthday is in the spring," he said, "when the river is always high and fast-flowing. Last year, it rained for days and days and days. On the morning of my birthday, I woke up to a splashing sound."

"Rain on the window?" asked Pickles in a bored voice.

"Water on the window, certainly," said Hoppity, "but it was lapping at the panes, not falling on them. The whole wood was flooded, right up to the second branch of our tree."

Penny was horrified. "What about all the poor rabbits underground?" she cried.

"Rabbits in Wilderness Wood are sensible and strong," said Hoppity. "They had all climbed up into the trunk of the tree and were busy making little boats out of everything they could find. As I looked out of the window, my great-grandmother sailed past in a suitcase. She had made a sail out of an old pair of her . . . *ahem*, well, bloomers."

The little rabbits giggled at the idea, but Pickles had more questions.

"What happened to all your presents?" he asked. He was thinking about the interesting packages that he knew were hiding under his parents' bed at that very moment.

"Luckily," said Hoppity, "they were the kind of presents that float. One by one, they came floating past my window, and I fished them out with my fishing rod. It was loads of fun, even if some of them were pretty soggy for a while. And my birthday cake never was seen again."

"I can see that it was exciting," said Pickles. "But why was it the best birthday ever?"

"Because of the whale," cried Hoppity, stretching his paws out wide. "A great big whale swam up the river and into the wood, and it got stuck between two trees."

Pickles was almost speechless. "A w-w-whale?" he gasped. "In Wilderness Wood? What happened to it?"

"We all made boats of everything we could find," said Hoppity, "as I explained. Then we sailed out and attached ropes to the whale. It was a tough job, but at last we managed to pull him out from between the trees and tow him back to the river and, eventually, the sea. It was the adventure of a lifetime, I can assure you. I can't imagine that anything as exciting as that happens in Warren Wood, does it?"

Pickles and Penny were silent. Nothing they had ever heard of even came close. It made the Party Problem seem pathetically small.

It was only later that night that Pickles began to think hard about that whale.

Next morning, he tackled Hoppity.

"There wasn't really a whale, was there?" he asked with a smile.

"Of course not," laughed Hoppity, "but it was a really good story, wasn't it? Now, what about a Deep Sea Party for your birthday?"

Pickles had to admit that was a pretty good idea. And Penny was as happy as could be, as she planned her mermaid costume.

Sister Susie-Sally's Tale of
THE FRIENDLY FOX

Pickles' big sister Susie-Sally was grown-up. She lived in a burrow on the other side of Warren Wood with her husband's family and her own baby rabbits. One afternoon, she came to visit her father and mother and to say hello to her baby brother. She found him playing in a clearing near the edge of the wood.

"Hello, Susa," called Pickles. When he was little, he couldn't say her full name, and his pet name for her had stuck.

Susie-Sally took her new responsibilities as a parent very seriously.

"Are you sure you should be playing all by yourself, young Pickles?" she asked. "You never know who might be lurking between the trees. What if there was a fox?"

"There hasn't been a fox in Warren Wood for ever so long," said Pickles, "and anyway, I don't think foxes are as bad as old rabbits say they are. I think they're like ogres and giants and goblins—they only really live in stories."

"I see," said his big sister. "Well, shall I tell you a story about a fox—a friendly fox?"

So as Susie-Sally led Pickles back to his home under the old oak tree, this is the story she told him.

"Once upon a time," she said, "there was a little rabbit who wouldn't do what his mother told him. He always had to find out for himself. If she told him not to touch a saucepan because it was hot, he would touch it anyway and burn his paws. When she told him not to go near the river, in case he fell in, he ran right to the edge of the bank and, of course . . . *splash!* . . . he was up to his ears in water. Luckily, two grown-up rabbits who were fishing nearby scooped him out—just in time."

Susie-Sally paused for breath. She could see that Pickles was listening intently.

"One day," she went on, "the little rabbit's mother told him to play indoors and, no matter what, not to wander out into the Wild Wood."

"But he did," Pickles squealed, "didn't he?"

"He did," said Susie-Sally solemnly, "and there he met a very friendly fox."

"I knew foxes were friendly," Pickles said. "What happened?"

"The fox was so friendly," said his big sister, "that he invited the little rabbit to see his den. That is what foxes call their homes, you know. They live underground, like us, though their rooms are not nearly as nice and they are not very good at housekeeping."

"Did he go?" asked Pickles. "The little rabbit, I mean. Did he go to the fox's den?"

"Yes, he went right along, and as the two of them trotted through the wood, the fox said, 'I especially wanted you to come for supper today. My family is really looking forward to it. Such a treat!'"

"How nice of the fox," said Pickles. "I wish I could meet him and visit his den."

"Not so fast, young Pickles. Wait till I tell you what happened to that little rabbit. He arrived at the fox's den and went inside. There were two little baby foxes there and a mother fox. And all of them smiled the biggest, toothiest smiles you have ever seen when they looked at the plump little rabbit. They were all just as friendly as the father fox had been."

"Did they play games?" asked Pickles.

"Yes, they played foxy games. They played Pounce and Push and they played Chase the Bunny and they played Catch."

"Those sound like good games," said Pickles.

"They were good games for foxes," agreed Susie-Sally darkly.

"So then they had supper?" asked her little brother. "What did they have for supper?"

"I hope you won't be upset, Pickles, but it was a tasty pie, made of something plump and furry."

Pickles was very quiet as they walked on.

"I know I shouldn't ask," he said at last. "But was it . . . I mean, it wasn't. . . . That is, you're not saying . . . are you?"

"I'm saying," said his sister, "that you should *always* do what your mother and father tell you, and you shouldn't trust strangers, no matter how friendly they seem. And more than that, I don't think I need to say. Do I?"

"No," agreed Pickles hastily. "You don't need to say anything else at all. I think I might play nearer home from now on. I must keep an eye on the younger rabbits, after all."

Mother Rabbit's Tale of
TOO MUCH FUDGE

Ⓞne afternoon, Pickles and Penny didn't feel very well. In fact, they felt so sick that their ears and whiskers drooped and they went to bed— while the sun was still shining.

Mother Rabbit was worried about her little ones. She asked them all kinds of questions about what might be wrong.

"Have you got colds?" she inquired. "Are there sniffles in your noses?"

"No, Mother," groaned Pickles.

"Did you play in the hot sun without your hats on? Are your ears aching?"

"No, Mother," moaned Penny.

"I may have to call Doctor Baggins," said Mother, "if you two don't feel better soon. I'll just go and get you each a glass of water."

But in the kitchen, Mother Rabbit saw something that made her change her mind about calling the doctor, and she didn't look quite so worried when she went back to the little rabbits.

"I'll just sit here and tell you a story," said Mother Rabbit, "and you can go to sleep and feel much better when you wake up."

"Once upon a time," said Mother Rabbit, "there were two little rabbits who always did what their mother told them. They were as good as gold. They wouldn't dream of hiding under the bed when it was time to wash the dishes. They always squeezed the toothpaste from the end of the tube. They never left dirty pawmarks in the bathroom. It was always a pleasure for their mother to look at her two little rabbits and say, 'My children are not silly like other bunnies. They are good, sensible young rabbits.'"

While Mother Rabbit was talking, quite a bit of wriggling and jiggling could be heard coming from two little bunnies in bed. Mother Rabbit smiled grimly.

"One day," she went on, "the little rabbits' mother was very busy in the kitchen. There was a Grand Fair the next day, and she had promised to bake some cakes for the cake stall. But when she looked in her cupboard, she found that she didn't have any eggs. She had no time to run out and buy some more, so she looked at the ingredients she did have to see if there was something else she could make. Pretty soon, she was melting all kinds of good things in a pan. A lovely smell came out of the kitchen, so that the two little rabbits came to see what was being cooked. The mother rabbit was stirring something with a big wooden spoon.

'This fudge isn't for you!' she laughed."

At that point, Mother Rabbit heard some shuffling and snuffling from her little rabbits. She smoothed down her apron and prepared to finish her story.

"By lunchtime," she said, "the mother rabbit had filled ten large tins with hot fudge. She put the pans on the kitchen table to cool. Of course, she knew that her little ones would never dream of tasting the delicious fudge. They knew that they must not eat sweet, sticky things between meals. So you can imagine how surprised she was when she came back from hanging out the laundry to find that two of the pans of fudge were missing. Obviously, she thought, someone had believed that she would not be able to count so many pans and might not notice that some were gone."

Now there was a deep silence from the two little rabbits. Mother Rabbit decided it was time to finish her story.

"Of course," she said, "it was very easy for the mother rabbit to find out who had stolen the fudge. Any rabbit would feel ill after eating a whole pan of sweet, sticky stuff. All she had to do was to visit all her friends and see who was looking a bit green around the whiskers. By the way, how are you two little bunnies feeling now? Any better? Or do I need to call Dr. Baggins?"

"No, no," cried Pickles and Penny, creeping out of their beds. "There's nothing wrong with us at all now. We feel fine!"

But you know, it's a strange thing, neither of those two little rabbits wanted anything for supper!

Half-Cousin Colly's Tale of
THE GHASTLY GHOST

Bunnies love to live together in big families. It doesn't matter how many brothers and sisters, aunts and uncles, cousins and half-cousins come along, there is always room for them. When everyone is starting to feel a little crowded, some grown-up rabbits just dig another couple of rooms so that all the bunnies can breathe again.

Bunnies enjoy living together so much that they don't usually feel the need to get away from it all, but they do love to visit their relatives in other burrows. One day, Pickles and his mother went to visit Half-Cousin Colly, who lived in a very ancient burrow under a wild, open heath. Pickles asked his mother to explain what a half-cousin was, but even after she had told him, he couldn't figure it out. All he knew was that Colly was a grown-up rabbit and he had once heard his granny say that he was eccentric. Pickles really didn't know what that meant either, so he had very little idea of what to expect.

The journey seemed to take forever.

It was growing dark when Pickles and his mother reached the entrance to Half-Cousin Colly's home. They decided at once that there was only one word to describe it. It was *spooky.*

"Why are there so many cobwebs?" whispered Pickles, clutching his mother's paw.

"Because there are so many spiders," said Mother Rabbit quietly. "Come on."

Mamma rang the bell, which clanged so loudly that Pickles, who was already feeling a little nervous, almost jumped out of his skin. The door opened with an ominous creak—all by itself! The two rabbits went in.

As the two bunnies walked slowly into the hallway, they suddenly felt very cold.

"I don't like it," wailed Pickles, burying his face in his mother's skirt. "It's scary!"

But just then, a cheerful voice called from a nearby room.

"Come on in, my dears! How lovely to see you!"

A jolly, plump rabbit in a bright red robe came towards them. It was Half-Cousin Colly.

After a delicious supper and lots of talk about family and friends, Pickles felt much better. Half-Cousin Colly was a friendly rabbit with lots of good stories to tell. Pickles forgot that he had ever been frightened in the large burrow.

But when it was time to go to bed, Colly showed Pickles to an enormous room with a big four-poster bed. The minute Colly shut the door with a cheery "Good night!" Pickles began to feel scared again.

Pickles lay awake in the silence, listening to his heart going *thump, thump, thump* in the darkness. It was not very long before he crept out of the room and slipped into his mother's bed, where it was warm and snug and safe.

"I know, Pickles," whispered Mother Rabbit, as she cuddled him. "There's something strange about this house. I'm just not quite sure what it is."

Next morning, the two bunnies met Half-Cousin Colly for breakfast. Mother Rabbit, who believed in sorting things out as soon as possible, spoke her mind.

"Colly," she said, "I'm afraid that both Pickles and I have felt uncomfortable in this house ever since we arrived. Is there something about it that you should tell us? It's almost as if it was . . . well, I don't like to say this, but . . . haunted."

Pickles almost fell off his chair when Half-Cousin Colly answered sadly, "Yes, this house is haunted. I share it with a ghastly ghost, and I suppose I should tell you about it."

"Is it a story suitable for a young bunny?" asked Mother Rabbit, preparing to cover Pickles' ears with her paws.

"It's something that every young bunny should know about," said Colly firmly. "There is a ghastly ghost that haunts every single part of this house. It is here all the time, day and night, but it is especially noticeable in the middle of the night. I have become so used to it that I hardly notice anymore. It is only when friends come to stay that I can see how uncomfortable they feel about it."

"Then you must do something about it," said Mother Rabbit briskly. "Ghosts can be dealt with, you know. Your home used to be so warm and inviting, full of laughing bunnies and. . ." Mother Rabbit broke off as she began to realize what Colly meant.

Half-Cousin Colly nodded his head. "I can see that you understand, my dear," he said. "The name of my ghastly ghost is loneliness. Since my wife passed away and my little ones went to homes of their own, this burrow has been so silent and lonely. It is far too big a burrow for one bunny like me, yet I cannot bring myself to leave the home where we once all lived so happily together."

"I think I have an idea," said Mother Rabbit with a smile. "Why not have other rabbits to stay? You are a wonderful cook and would make everyone so welcome. Rabbits on their way to another place or rabbits who wanted a break from their usual burrows would love to come, I'm sure."

And that is why, if you visit Half-Cousin Colly's Bunny Bed and Breakfast today (though I hear he is booked up months ahead!) you will find a very different kind of burrow. And as for the loneliness ghost, it has gone right away, and that is the only guest that Half-Cousin Colly *won't* be inviting back!

Aunt Prettypaws' Tale of RIBBONS AND LACE

One day you may be lucky enough to get an invitation to a bunny wedding. If you do, please, *please* accept it, for no one knows how to celebrate like bunnies do. They will throw a party for any tiny thing, so you can imagine that a wedding is a very big event. The singing, dancing, feasting, and fun go on for days and days.

Although Pickles and Penny loved to go and join in the merrymaking, they were not very interested in hearing stories about weddings. There is always a lot to organize when two bunnies get married, and the little rabbits knew that elderly aunts in particular just love to tell you all about the hundreds of weddings they have helped to make occasions to remember.

Aunt Prettypaws was like that. She didn't visit very often, but when she did she was always busy embroidering some frilly scrap of material or threading ribbons through a wedding shawl. When Aunt Prettypaws was around, Pickles and Penny often tried not to be!

But one morning, when the snow was too deep on the ground for little bunnies to hop, Pickles and Penny found themselves shut up in the living room with Aunt Prettypaws.

Penny untangled a bag of ribbon for the old bunny, while Pickles found that it was fun to look through Aunt Prettypaws' workbag. And that is how they came to hear the tale of ribbons and lace.

"I'm sure you know, young bunnies," Aunt Prettypaws began, "that it is the custom for bunny brides to make their own wedding dresses. And the days are long gone when a simple gown would do. Oh no, nowadays brides must wear as many ribbons and frills as they can."

"My cousin Mabel could hardly move," said Penny, remembering how she had had to help to push the bride through a narrow doorway, tucking her frilly skirts around her.

"Well, that is probably going too far," smiled Aunt Prettypaws. "But the bride I am thinking of almost didn't go far enough."

"What happened?" asked Penny.

"Well, Letitia was a lovely young bunny in every way, but she was always busy. She looked after baby bunnies in the mornings. She helped her father in his digging business in the afternoons. And in between, she was the leading light of most of the clubs and societies in Warren Wood. And that is why, I'm sorry to say, she put off making her wedding dress until the very, very, last moment."

"Didn't she have time to finish it?" asked Penny, who thought she could see where this story would end. She giggled as she imagined a bride dressed only in her petticoat and veil.

"Oh, it wasn't that," said Aunt Prettypaws. "Letitia left herself just enough time to finish sewing the dress. No, her problem came when she went to old Mr. Bobbin's shop to buy her ribbons and lace. For the shop was closed, and a big sign on the door said 'AWAY ON BUSINESS. BACK NEXT MONTH.'"

"So she had no ribbons and no lace?" asked Pickles, winding some ribbon around his paws. "What did she do next, Auntie?"

"She cried," sighed Aunt Prettypaws. "Yes, she sat down on a tree stump in Warren Wood and sobbed. She thought her wedding dress would be ruined, and she had so wanted to look lovely on her special day. But as she sat there, her old granny happened to come along."

"Did she have some ribbons and lace?" asked Penny.

"No," said Aunt Prettypaws, "but she had a very good idea. She told Letitia not to worry and went off to see her friends deep in the wood. She knew they would help."

"Did they have a shop too?" asked Pickles.

"No, they were not bunnies at all. They were little woodland creatures so tiny you often don't even see them as you walk by their workshops. Yes, Granny went to talk to the spiders, who can spin lace so fine and beautiful that no bunny can match it. Then she visited the little birds who hop along the hedges. She had a special job for them, you see."

"For a whole week, the spiders were spinning their delicate lace and the little birds were gathering rose petals and threading them together to make long pink ribbons. Then they carried the lovely things they had made to Granny."

"Was there time to sew them all onto the dress?" asked Penny, who found that sewing took a long time.

"There was just enough time," smiled Aunt Prettypaws, "and everyone said that Letitia's dress was the prettiest they had ever seen."

"I'd like my wedding dress to have spider lace and rose-petal ribbons," sighed Penny, which made Pickles groan and hide his head in Aunt Prettypaws' workbag!

Baby Honeybun's Tale of
The Talking Toy

Penny and Pickles had never been so bored. Mother Rabbit had asked them to watch Baby Honeybun while she went shopping.

"Don't leave her alone even for a moment," warned Mother. "Babies can get into all sorts of trouble before you know it. The time will fly by. Baby Honeybun is sure to keep you entertained."

But Baby Honeybun didn't do anything. First she slept for a long time, wiggling her little nose when Pickles leaned close to make sure she was still breathing.

"I thought babies cried all the time," said Penny, "but Baby Honeybun doesn't make a sound. I almost wish she would."

As if she had heard Penny, Baby Honeybun suddenly woke up and gave two big sneezes. They were such large sneezes coming from a tiny bunny that even Baby Honeybun herself looked shocked and shook her little whiskers to and fro.

"Maybe now she'll play with us," said Pickles. "Here, Baby! Chase Uncle Pickles!"

But Baby Honeybun just sat looking up at Pickles. She didn't move at all.

"Can she walk?" asked Pickles.

"I don't think so." Penny shook her head. "But I think she can roll around on her tummy."

"Well, she's not doing it now," said Pickles. "She's not doing anything at all. I didn't realize that babies were so *boring*. I bet I wasn't like this when I was little. Do something, Baby!"

Baby Honeybun blinked. She wiggled her nose. She gave a big sigh. And she went straight back to sleep, snuggled into a cushion on the floor.

Now anyone who has ever looked after a bunny baby—or any baby, for that matter—for any length of time will know that sleeping is a Good Thing. While a baby is sleeping, she isn't crawling into the coal scuttle or pulling off her clothes or doing any one of the hundreds of things that babies do so well.

But Penny didn't know much about babies, and that is why she made a Really Big Mistake. She nudged Baby Honeybun's toe to wake her up.

Baby Honeybun stirred, as though she didn't quite believe what she had felt.

Penny nudged her gently again.

Baby Honeybun opened one eye. There was no doubt about it.

She looked angry. In fact, she looked angrier than any baby bunny Pickles and Penny had ever seen. Then Baby Honeybun opened her little pink mouth and began to yell.

It wasn't a quiet, unhappy kind of yell. It wasn't a medium-sized, slightly annoyed kind of yell. It was a huge, I-am-furious kind of yell, and it didn't stop.

Baby Honeybun yelled and yelled and yelled. Her little face grew pinker and pinker, and tiny tears ran down her furry cheeks.

"What should I do?" cried Penny. "I didn't mean to upset her!"

"Maybe she's hungry," suggested Pickles. "We could give her some milk." He always found a snack was helpful in a crisis.

"No, no," cried Penny. "She has a special kind and I don't know where it is. We don't want to poison her, too!"

"We could pick her up and cuddle her," suggested Pickles.

"You try," said Penny. "I'm not going to touch her again. Look what happened last time."

Very, very carefully, Pickles picked up the screaming baby. She was surprisingly heavy.

"Ouch!" yelled Pickles. And he put the baby back onto her cushion as quickly as he could. "She kicked me!" he squealed.

"We'll have to try singing," said Penny. And she launched into a rousing chorus of "Five Little Bunnies" before Pickles could stop her.

It didn't seem possible that Baby Honeybun could yell any louder, but she did. At the sound of the song, she made an extra-special effort, and her pink face went purple with rage.

Penny was almost in tears herself now. But she had no more ideas.

"We could tell her a story," said Pickles. "Once upon a time, there was a little baby bunny called Baby Honeybun. . . ."

Baby Honeybun's yells became a tiny fraction quieter.

". . .she lived in a burrow with her two best friends, Penny and Pickles," Penny went on.

Baby Honeybun's yells increased again.

"No, no, she didn't," said Pickles hastily. "She lived in a burrow with. . ."

Baby Honeybun threw her blue bunny toy across the room.

"She lived in a burrow with a cuddly blue bunny and. . ."

Baby Honeybun threw her pink butterfly rattle across the room.

". . .and a noisy pink butterfly," said Pickles, who was beginning to get the hang of this. "One day," he went on, "something really terrible happened to Baby Honeybun. She was left all alone with two big monsters, called Penny and Pickles. And they were *horrible*!"

Baby Honeybun stopped yelling for a moment and made a kind of gurgling noise. It was almost as if she was laughing.

"Those horrible monsters did awful things," said Pickles. "They grabbed her and nearly dropped her. They made a terrible squeaky noise at her. And they woke her up when she was having a nice, quiet nap in the afternoon."

Baby Honeybun sighed again. For a whole two minutes she had forgotten to yell.

"The worst thing was," said Pickles, "that the monsters couldn't understand baby talk at all. This made Baby Honeybun so angry that all she could do was yell. Then she had a very good idea. She remembered that her cuddly blue bunny could speak lots of different languages, so she whispered in his ear what she wanted to say to the horrible monsters."

Pickles gently held the blue bunny close to Baby Honeybun. Then he held it up to his own furry ear.

"Is that so?" he asked, listening hard to the blue bunny. "Well, that is fine. Penny, please be quiet. Baby Honeybun wants to have a little nap."

And at that, Baby Honeybun gave a big yawn and closed her eyes.

When Mother Rabbit came back from her shopping a few minutes later, she found not one but *three* sleeping bunnies in her living room. And she was far too sensible to wake *any* of them.

Great-Grandpa Bill's Tale of

HOW THINGS USED TO BE

Great-Grandpa Bill cleared his throat. He was about to tell a story. As quietly as they could, several rabbits slipped out of the room and several others settled down for a little snooze. They had all heard Great-Grandpa's stories many, many times before, and it was very warm with so many bunnies sitting around the fire.

"When I was a young rabbit," said Great-Grandpa Bill, "things were very hard. We didn't have all the comforts that you young rabbits take for granted today. We didn't have any electricity or running water indoors. We had to go outside, even on the coldest days, and carry heavy buckets of water from the well. It wasn't an easy job, I can tell you, especially in the middle of winter when the well was frozen solid."

"What's a well?" asked a little voice from the back, only to be silenced by lots of "Shhhhhhhhs" from other bunnies. It took Great-Grandpa Bill long enough to tell his stories without little ones interrupting and making him lose his thread.

"We were very poor," Great-Grandpa Bill went on, causing another handful of bunnies to doze off, "and we had hardly any toys to play with. We had to make our own entertainment in those days. That's when I learned to juggle. Pass me those carrots, young Pickles."

Pickles passed the carrots, but several other bunnies slipped out of the room or down behind the sofa. The one thing that everyone knew about Great-Grandpa Bill's juggling was that he wasn't very good at it. True to form, in the next few minutes, he managed to break the glass in a picture frame and knock over a vase of flowers, soaking several bunnies in the process.

·"And that's another thing," the old rabbit went on, chewing thoughtfully on one of his juggling carrots, "things in those days were made to last. They didn't tip over or fall apart like the flimsy things of today."

Two bunnies silently scuttled around clearing up the mess, as Great-Grandpa Bill droned on. More and more of his listeners were finding that his voice made them feel extraordinarily tired.

"Bunnies today have an easy life," said Grandpa. "Washing machines, vacuum cleaners, central heating . . . we didn't have any of those in the old days. But then, rabbits were made of sterner stuff then. Nowadays, most young rabbits couldn't do a hard day's work to save their lives. They've become soft."

Several bunnies who had so far only closed their eyes, now closed their ears as well. They had heard it all before.

Great-Grandpa Bill talked on for another half hour. He spoke of the difficulties of storing carrots in the days before refrigeration. He mused on the shortcomings of modern rabbits who no longer knew how to make their own soap. He remembered several rabbits in the past who had all expressed undying admiration for Great-Grandpa Bill.

At this point, the old rabbit called rather tetchily for a glass of water for his poor old throat. Years of pulling carrots in the frosty mornings of his youth had left him with a weakness in the vocal passages, he said. Poor Great-Grandma Lill shuffled off to bring him refreshments. She had heard his stories so many times before that she went onto automatic pilot as soon as Great-Grandpa Bill began clearing his throat.

"Ah, now, that's better," said the storyteller, taking a sip of water, "though it's not as good and cold as well-water used to be. Now, where was I?

Oh yes, I was just coming to the really exciting part of my story. It concerns the time I met a ferocious tiger in the woods."

Great-Grandpa Bill looked around expectantly. He expected a sharp intake of breath from his listeners as he gave this surprising news. But there was not a sound from anyone, except a very gentle snore from Great-Grandma Lill, who had held out longer than the rest of the sleeping audience.

Great-Grandpa Bill poked the fire in disgust. "It's just as I thought," he said. "Rabbits nowadays have no stamina. None at all."

Great-Grandma Guggles and THE TALE THAT NEVER ENDS

Great-Grandma Guggles sat down on the grass, surrounded by several of her little great-grandchildren, and began her story.

"Once upon a time," she said, "there was a young gentleman rabbit and a young lady rabbit who settled down together in a big family burrow in Warren Wood. Before long, they had five little baby bunnies. And goodness me, those babies were a trouble to their parents. They squiggled and wriggled all over the place."

"Like us?" asked the little bunnies, squiggling and wriggling themselves.

"Just like you," smiled Grandma Guggles. "But very, very slowly, the baby bunnies grew up. Soon they could ride their bicycles and write their own names all by themselves."

"We'll be able to do that soon," squeaked the little bunnies.

"Yes, indeed," agreed Great Grandma Guggles, "and pretty soon after that, you'll be almost grown-up and causing your parents all sorts of trouble all over again."

"What sort of trouble?" asked the little rabbits.

"Motorcycles," muttered the old lady darkly, "and short skirts and loud music. It's always the same with rabbits when they're nearly grown."

"Then what happens?" asked the little rabbits.

"Well, I don't know for sure what will happen to *you*," their great-grandmother went on, "but in this particular family, pretty soon those little rabbits were grown up and courting."

"Courting? What's courting?" asked one little rabbit curiously.

"I know," squeaked another. "It's lovey-dovey stuff and kissing and cuddling and not wanting little rabbits around."

"*Oooooh noooo!*" squealed the other bunnies. "We won't want to do that, not *ever*!"

"Well, I'm not so sure," said Great Grandma Guggles. "These rabbits I'm talking about, two by two they soon started wanting to settle down together in a big family burrow in Warren Wood. And before long, they had. . ."

"Baby bunnies! We know!" cried the little ones.

But Great Grandma Guggles shook her head. "These baby bunnies were special," she smiled. "These baby bunnies were *you*!"